WHAT TO DO WHEN
CLIMATE
CHANGE
SCARES YOU

A Kid's Guide to Dealing With Climate Change Stress

by **Leslie Davenport**

illustrated by
Irma Ruggiero

Magination Press • Washington, DC
American Psychological Association

This book is dedicated to our kids:

The ones under our roof, those we guide in classrooms, and the ones we love from afar.

Our kids who are full of curiosity, honesty, challenges, bravery, and dreams, who are growing so fast and who feel everything.

Our kids whom we cherish and are so proud of, whose movements we track with our hearts.

Our kids who will live in a very different future than the one we used to imagine.

We ask their forgiveness for leaving them a world whose climates, landscapes, and inhabitants have been, at times, so disregarded, dismissed, and damaged.

We're learning and changing, too. We're here. We're with you.

Let's make things better together—*LD*

To Lara, always by my side—*IR*

Books for Kids From the
American Psychological Association

Magination Press is a registered trademark of the American Psychological Association. Order books at maginationpress.org or call 1-800-374-2721.

Book design by Christina Gaugler
Printed by Sheridan-Worzalla, Stevens Point, WI

Library of Congress Cataloging-in-Publication Data

Names: Davenport, Leslie (Climate psychology educator and consultant), author. | Ruggiero, Irma, illustrator.

Title: What to do when climate change scares you : a kid''s guide to dealing with climate change stress / by Leslie Davenport ; illustrated by Irma Ruggiero.

Description: Washington, DC : Magination Press, [2025] | Series: What-to-do guides for kids series | Summary: ""An activity workbook to help children cope with anxiety about climate change"— Provided by publisher.

Identifiers: LCCN 2024007840 (print) | LCCN 2024007841 (ebook) | ISBN 9781433844829 (paperback) | ISBN 9781433844836 (ebook)

Subjects: LCSH: Stress management for children—Juvenile literature. | Stress (Psychology)—Juvenile literature. | Environmental psychology—Juvenile literature. | Climatic changes—Juvenile literature. | Global warming—Juvenile literature. | Sustainability—Juvenile literature. | BISAC: JUVENILE NONFICTION / Science & Nature / Environmental Conservation & Protection | JUVENILE NONFICTION / Health & Daily Living / Mental Health

Classification: LCC BF723.S75 D38 2025 (print) | LCC BF723.S75 (ebook) | DDC 155.4/189042—dc23/eng/20240323
LC record available at https://lccn.loc.gov/2024007840
LC ebook record available at https://lccn.loc.gov/2024007841
Manufactured in the United States of America

10 9 8 7 6 5 4 3 2 1

CONTENTS

NOTE TO PARENTS AND CAREGIVERS

Perhaps more than anything else, we want children to feel and be safe. It's a natural instinct to want to protect them from the harsher realities of life. However, climate change poses a very real and ongoing threat. Your family may have already experienced bigger storms and hotter summers or had to stay indoors due to smoky, unhealthy air. Maybe you've had to evacuate from wildfires or floods. Unfortunately, climate scientists are warning us that these kinds of climate change impacts are going to increase in the years ahead. When faced with any of these difficult events, children want and need to understand why their lives may be changing. The ongoing threats to our communities are real, and it makes sense when both kids and adults become concerned about climate change. In fact, feelings of distress are a sign that we care about the well-being of life on Earth.

Even if you live in an area that hasn't undergone severe impacts from climate change, kids are besieged with news about it from television, car radios, friends, social media, and overheard adult conversations that often describe the most extreme weather events. Powerful images of destruction and hearing from people traumatized by a climate event can lead children to make wrong assumptions about the immediate dangers for them and their family.

Many schools are beginning to introduce a climate curriculum into their classrooms, but it doesn't typically include coping tools to support the feelings that can be triggered when kids learn what it means to live in a warming world. The disappearing glaciers and how that devastates polar bears and other arctic wildlife; the decline in bee and other insect populations and the effect of that on the food cycle; and the myriad forms of suffering that climate change is visiting on people, land, other animals, and cultures: It's not surprising that children may become frightened or confused. Kids need help to put climate change into perspective and feel supported in their individual and family lives.

While you can't fix climate change for your child, you can help them discover the facts, know they're not alone, and find ways to take action together. It really matters to kids how the important adults in their lives respond to their concerns. If their caregiver avoids the topic, it makes them more anxious. Seeing adults working to protect and care for the Earth and prioritizing sustainable actions carries a powerful message to kids. This is an opportunity to not only provide good parenting but also to continue your own personal discovery of eco-wise living and how to live more sustainably.

Climate change is a challenging subject for most adults, too, and entering into family discussions may multiply your own complex feelings. Remember that children are affected by the emotions of those around them, especially family. While you want to acknowledge and validate the feelings that climate change can trigger in your child, you don't want to process your feelings with them. It's important that you also have supportive adults to talk to. Don't let your own fears lead to sharing your speculations about the future. Think of ways you can take care of your own emotions so you can be available for your children. Can you do something like go for a walk or talk to a friend before talking to your children? If you don't already have support, consider talking with other parents about how they cope or joining an organization that offers family-oriented environmental education and projects in the community.

It's also helpful to brush up on climate science, and there are many reliable resources on-line such as NASA and National Geographic Kids. But what's more important than knowing all the answers are the ways you can connect with your child throughout the exploration. Caring for the environment can become a valuable and ongoing conversation. Read through this book first to familiarize yourself with the ideas and exercises presented. When you start the conversation about climate change, ask your child what they know and how they feel about the topic. You might be surprised to learn how much they've already heard, including unfounded misperceptions that need to be corrected. Give your child your full attention, and listen closely to their feelings, questions, and hopes. Without minimizing their worries, let them know that you care about the future of the Earth, too. If they're frightened, you can express something like this: "I know that climate change is big and it can feel overwhelming,but I also know that there's so much we can do to make a difference. Let's read this book together. I don't have all the answers, but I know it's a very important subject and we can learn together. Let's keep talking: I like to hear what you're feeling and thinking. Let's set up a regular time to do this." Tell the truth gently. Rather than lecturing, make sure that your answers are in response to what your child is curious about. Follow their lead, paying attention to when they need a break from the topic. It's most effective to provide information in small doses, giving them time to take it in and think about it. And be sure to read together about the many wonderful people and organizations working every day to reverse climate change.

Climate psychology understands that addressing eco-anxiety in kids and adults has two core components: validating and learning ways to deal directly with emotional distress, and finding out how to take action and become part of creating a safer, healthier world. *What to Do When Climate Change Scares You* provides you and your child with step-by-step guidance and exercises in both of these areas. As you learn together, you'll discover the importance of social/environmental justice. As greener policies are being developed at all levels of government, meaningful change needs to prioritize the fair treatment of all people, regardless of color, national origin, or income. This is explored in kid-friendly terms in Chapter Six.

Climate change has unfortunately become an inevitable part of life, and this book can guide your efforts to help kids navigate the present and future challenges more successfully. But focusing on the exploration as a family offers the possibility of much more than improved coping. There remains the very real need and opportunity to rise to what's perhaps the greatest challenge in our history. We want to leave our children the legacy of a better world than the one we inherited. We all have a role to play in driving the cultural shift toward a healthier world—and when enough people work together, we can make a significant difference in our children's future.

CHAPTER 1

Your Feelings About a Changing Planet

Ready to start a learning adventure and discover more about yourself and our beautiful planet?

You'll be zooming out into space and peeking up close at the plants and animals to learn more about how climate change is warming up our world. And you'll be exploring your feelings and finding out how to care for this amazing place called Earth where we all live.

To prepare for your travels, let's gather some important supplies.

Write or draw some other things in the backpack that you think would be good to bring on your learning journey.

When you hear that the climate is changing, you might not understand what that means or how it might affect you. This can make kids worry that something bad is going to happen to them.

Worries and fears are natural: Everyone worries about different things at different times, including adults.

When it comes to climate change, the worry is called **eco-anxiety**. "Eco" means the environment, all the living things on our Earth, and "anxiety" is fear or worry.

When you feel this way and experience eco-anxiety, it means that you're a smart and aware person: You've been paying attention to what's happening in the world, and you care about all the people, animals, and green growing things on our beautiful planet.

Of course, we want to take care of the things we love that are important to us, like our family, friends, pets, and favorite places and things. Taking care of the Earth and everything on it makes sense: It helps us keep things safe and healthy for everyone. And that feels good!

On this journey, you'll be discovering ways that you can make a difference to our Earth and our environment.

Write or draw some things you love about nature, being outdoors, and our Earth.

It might be swimming in a lake, seeing colorful flowers, the smell of rain, camping, watching the clouds, outdoor sports, or the taste of a fresh peach. What do you love and enjoy the most?

Here, write or draw what you want to learn about climate change.

What have you heard about climate change? Are you curious about how the climate is changing? Or what people are doing about it?

Last, **write or draw** any worries and other feelings you might have about our warming world.

Are you upset that some people have had floods or wildfires in their communities? Are you sad for the animals who lost their homes? Are you afraid of the things that might happen in your neighborhood? This is a good place to start naming your worries. In the chapters ahead, you'll be learning about some great tools that will help you with eco-anxiety and other feelings.

CHAPTER 2

What is Climate Change?

You packed your imagination to take on this trip, so let's use it right now. Let's zoom out and learn about the Earth's atmosphere.

The atmosphere is a blanket of different gases that surrounds our planet. It's 300 miles thick, and the part we breathe is about 60 miles! It keeps us warm, protects us from outer space, gives us oxygen to breathe, and it's where our weather begins.

Science helps us understand our world, but nature can also give us lots of feelings. Nature can even tell us something about ourselves. Let's come back and put our feet on the ground and see what nature has to show us.

Let's visit your first heart from Chapter One, the one that is full of happy nature feelings... like when you watch the moon and stars come out at night, hear a river or ocean, see a rainbow, or smell the first flowers blooming in Spring.

Let's bring some nature inside, by making a **nature art picture.**

My Nature Art Picture

1. Take a small bag or cup with you and **collect** at least six small things from outside, like a shell, twig, rock, dry flower, moss, or acorn.

   Pick things that have different colors, some that are soft and hard, some that are light and heavier. You can also use pictures or drawings of your favorite things from nature instead.

2. Once you have collected your nature art items or pictures, begin to **arrange** them on a piece of paper in any way you want. You can stack them, spread them out, have them touching or apart.

3. Once you have them just right for now, **give your picture a title.**

4. You can keep your nature items or pictures in a cup or bowl, change them, add to them, and arrange them again in different ways any time you want.

How do you feel making art with nature?

_____

_____

Why did you pick each object?

_____

_____

Why did you pick that title?

_____

_____

Can you think of a feeling to go with each object?

_____

_____

What other things did you see, feel, or notice while you
were gathering them?

_____

_____

Now let's get back to the atmosphere, and learn a little more about our warming world.

One of the important gases in the atmosphere is **carbon dioxide**; it's also called CO_2. It keeps the temperature of our atmosphere "not too hot" and "not too cold."

Scientists tell us that for almost 800,000 years, the amount of CO_2 in the atmosphere stayed about the same. But around the year 1950, things began to change. The amount of CO_2 started to grow, and it's still growing—and that's the main cause of climate change.

The problem is that when there's too much CO_2, extra heat gets trapped in the atmosphere, and that makes things on Earth start changing. Here are a few examples:

► The extra heat melts the ice caps on the Earth's north and south poles and the glaciers up in the mountains, and that makes it harder for animals that need snow and cold, like polar bears and Arctic foxes.

► Some areas have floods, because on some parts of the planet, warmer temperatures mean more rain, and because, as the ice and glaciers melt, the oceans rise higher onto the Earth's shores.

► Some places get too hot and dry, and that can mean more wildfires.

Learning about the ways that climate change makes it harder for people, animals, and plants stirs up eco-anxiety, because we want our world to be safe and healthy. This brings us to your third heart in Chapter One, where you wrote your feelings. You may feel eco-anxiety in many ways.

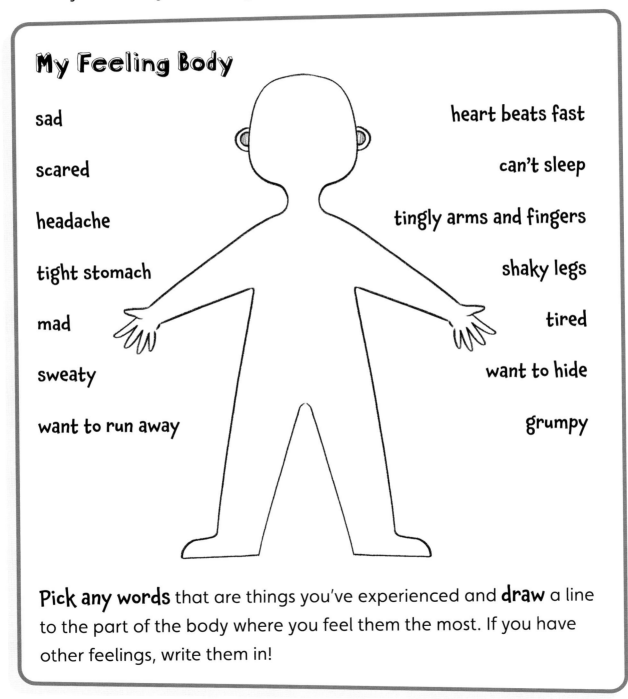

My Feeling Body

sad

scared

headache

tight stomach

mad

sweaty

want to run away

heart beats fast

can't sleep

tingly arms and fingers

shaky legs

tired

want to hide

grumpy

Pick any words that are things you've experienced and **draw** a line to the part of the body where you feel them the most. If you have other feelings, write them in!

The main reason that there's too much CO_2 in the atmosphere is the pollution caused by burning **fossil fuels**—the gasoline, coal, and oil that our factories, cars, power plants, and airplanes use.

There are other things that hurt nature too, like littering and cutting down all the trees.

But the good news is, that's not the end of the story. Governments, scientists, and many people like you and me are looking for earth-friendly ways to make changes so that fossil fuels can't do any more damage to the atmosphere.

You've probably heard of some of those changes: solar, wind, hydroelectric, and electric power. Community tree planting and litter clean-up days help too. This helps keep our air and water clean and helps keep the earth from getting too hot.

Write or draw what a safer, healthier world would look like when we use less fossil fuel and use more clean energy.

Have you seen any of these earth-friendly changes near you? Have you seen solar panels on a neighbor's house or office building? Have you spotted any wind turbines? Maybe you've seen a poster announcing a litter pick up day in your community.

Imagining the possibilities of how the Earth can be healthier is an important part of making helpful changes. As you continue reading this book, you'll be learning more and more tools to put these ideas into action.

CHAPTER 3

Changing Feelings About a Changing World

When you start learning about climate change, it can stir up a lot of worry, and that's normal.

But sometimes your fears about climate change don't match what's really happening in the world.

For example: Maybe you hear about a hurricane in another state, and you start to be concerned that your own house, apartment, or school is going to get flooded.

Or you remember a day last summer when the air was smoky from a nearby forest fire, and you wonder if you and the people and things you care about are ever going to be safe.

When you think a lot about one thing—like climate change—it can make your worry grow bigger than what's really happening, and that can make it seem like the *only* thing that's happening.

Understanding and fixing climate change is a very important job for everyone, especially people in governments and big companies. Our job as kids and adults is to understand climate change so that we can live a good life and be part of making things better.

If you're worrying too much about climate change, one way to get your mind and feelings back in balance is to take a few minutes and notice some of the ordinary things that are happening in your life. These activities might be fun, boring, exciting...or just ordinary.

Here are some examples of ordinary or fun things:

► You went to school

► It's a great day to be outside

► The library is open and you got a new book

► You saw a friend and said hi

► You're eating a good snack

Write or draw a picture of something you noticed or did today that was fun or ordinary. Add more if you have more!

Spend a few more minutes thinking of some of the things you did and some of the good and ordinary things that happened today, yesterday, this week, or even this month.

When you're worried because you don't know what's going to happen in the future, you can get frightened—and then the **What-Ifs** come.

Worried + Unknown Future = What-Ifs!

Both kids and adults sometimes have to deal with the What-Ifs. Your mind wants to figure it all out, but it doesn't have all the facts, so it starts making up worry stories.

These stories can make you more frightened than you need to be, because they don't always tell the truth: They want you to believe that the worst possible thing is *definitely* going to happen!

► What if...there's a fire in my community?

► What if...my pet gets lost in a flood?

► What if...we run out of water from the drought?

It's bedtime, but Emma feels too upset to sleep. She tells her mom about a TV news story she saw about a family's home that flooded. The reporter talked about a big storm and the rising sea level.

Emma asks her mom, "What if...the ocean floods our home while I'm sleeping?"

Her mom listens to Emma's feelings and concerns, and she tells Emma that she understands and is glad they're talking about it. Then she gives Emma a big hug.

Her mom tells Emma that she's very interested in climate change and how to make the world a safer place for their family and everyone else.

She explains that their home is far enough away from the ocean to be safe from flooding.

She asks Emma if tomorrow morning she'd like to learn more about the rising sea level. They also talk about the steps that community leaders are taking to keep the community safe from the effects of climate change.

Emma feels a little calmer knowing that her parents know a lot about climate change and are working to protect her.

The next day Emma and her parents go to the library and find two books and one website about the rising sea level and climate change.

Emma's dad also shows her where their house is on a map and explains how they live at a safe distance from the ocean.

They talk about a project that they're helping with on the shore in a nearby town that will help keep back any flood waters and protect ocean fish.

While climate change can be scary, it's important to understand exactly what's going on, especially when it's upsetting you. It's always important to know the facts! That makes it easier to plan, prepare, and make good choices.

It also helps us understand what we need to do to stop climate change.

You can learn to be smarter and stronger than the What-Ifs by finding out the facts, just like Emma. First, talk to an adult who can help you find out more information about your climate-change fear.

Write down two adults who can help you learn the facts that scientists have discovered about your specific concern. One of them might be the person who gave you this book.

1. _____

2. _____

Do some research on your topic! Put your findings in a What-If chart. Take a look at Emma's chart to see how it's done.

MY WHAT-IF WORRY	*What if my house floods from sea level rising because of climate change.*
WHAT I LEARNED ABOUT IT	*Sea level rising happens slowly over a period of many years in certain places. My house is not close in an area that will be touched by rising seas.*
THESE FACTS ARE FROM (BOOK, WEBSITE, TEACHER...)	*A map of my town and state that my Dad showed me. He pointed out where we live.* *NASA Kids website.* *Two books on climate change from the library.*
I FEEL	*I feel calmer that I can sleep safely in my house. I also feel excited to learn more about how I can help stop the warming and sea level rise.*

Now fill out your **What-If** chart!

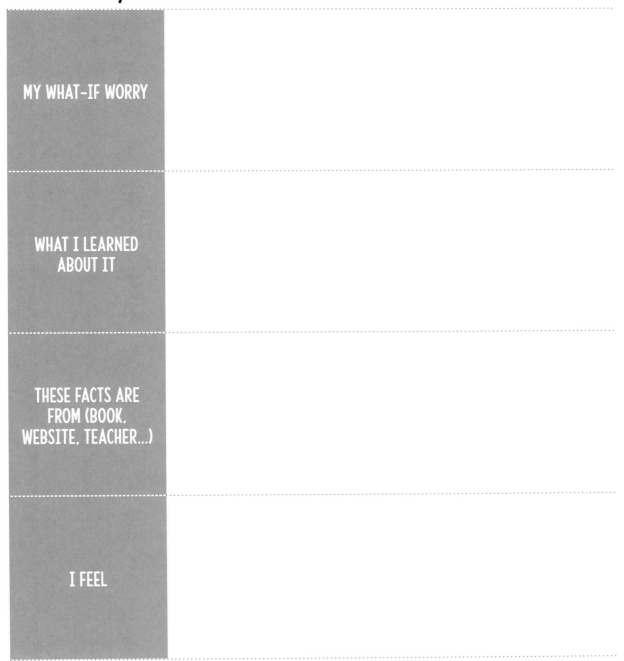

MY WHAT-IF WORRY	
WHAT I LEARNED ABOUT IT	
THESE FACTS ARE FROM (BOOK, WEBSITE, TEACHER...)	
I FEEL	

When you **fill in** your What-If chart, notice how you feel after you've learned more of the facts compared to when you were focusing on your fear.

Feelings are normal, and it's okay to have all kinds of feelings. You probably have many different feelings every day, and as you learn more ways to understand and work with them, you'll discover that there are ways to feel stronger and calmer more of the time.

Let's add to your "eco-smart" backpack, starting with all the things that you already know to do when you want to feel calmer.

What are some things you like to do to feel relaxed or have fun? Circle ones that you do!

skateboarding

taking a deep breath

reading

drawing

playing with a friend

playing a sport

listening to music

Write down any other things you like to do!

_____

_____

_____

_____

_____

You'll learn lots of other ways to to outsmart the What-Ifs as we continue our journey. Like:

► In Chapter Seven, you'll learn what to do in an emergency. Even before climate change, it's always been smart to know what to do in case of a fire, flood, earthquake, or any kind of surprising situation. You'll learn about how you, your community, and your country can be prepared and stay safe.

► Be a part of stopping climate change. There are lots of ways to join with adults and other kids who're working to create a safer and healthier world for everyone.

CHAPTER 4

Being a Change-Maker

Life is always changing. Can you remember the first time you tasted ice cream, or your first day of school?

Every time we experience something in the world around us, like trying a new dessert or learning to ride a bike, we also have a matching experience inside: our feelings. When you learn to ride a bike, you might feel excited, scared, or frustrated—and when you're finally whizzing around the park, you feel happy!

Climate change is changing our home, the Earth, and so naturally we have lots of feelings about that too.

First let's help ourselves with our climate change feelings—and then we'll learn about helping to make the world healthier.

Feelings can be our buddies that help us understand ourselves and the world and learn the right ways to act. For example, when we're afraid, fear is letting us know that some kind of change is happening.

Fear tells us to be aware of what's happening, take care of ourselves, and stay safe.

Sad feelings can help us see and understand what we wish was different.

When something doesn't seem fair, we can feel mad—and that feeling can help us work toward finding a better solution.

Color in the plants that name a feeling that you've experienced. You might think of other feelings you've had, and you can write them on the plants that don't have feeling names on them. **Write under that plant** what happened that led up to those feelings.

My Feeling Garden

You might also feel more than one feeling at once. If you've done a sport competition or art performance, maybe you've felt both nervous and excited. Or if you worked on a tough school project, you might have felt frustrated but also proud. Can you think of a situation where you felt two feelings at once? You can write two feelings in one flower for those situations!

Every fun or challenging change that you've experienced in your life helps you be more prepared for the next one. And you've already had lots of useful experiences! **Circle the changes** you've experienced in your life and **write in** more that you remember.

Great! Now we're going to explore some of the ways our warming world is changing. Do any of these sound familiar?

► smoky skies from a forest fire

► sports field flooded

► pollution in your favorite lake or river

► trash on the road or beach

► or something else?

If you've had an experience like this, it can be helpful to write about it. If you haven't, pull out the imagination from your backpack and imagine what it might feel like.

What was hard about the change?

Did anything help you feel better about the hard parts?

What did you learn?

How do you feel about the change now?

Each thing you experience—especially when you make it through the tough parts—can help you build new skills, become smarter, and be more confident in navigating your life. It can also give you energy to be part of helping make the world healthier. Being part of making the world a better place feels good too!

There are lots of young people like you around the world taking action to help the planet.

Meet Mari

Mari Copeny, also known as "Little Miss Flint," was very upset that lots of people in her community of Flint, Michigan were drinking polluted water. Poisonous chemicals like lead were leaking out of old pipes in the city's water system that should have been repaired years before. The water was brown when it came out of the faucet, and lots of people—especially kids—got sick.

When Mari was eight years old, she learned about this serious health problem in her city and she wanted to fix it.

She wrote a letter to President Barack Obama. President Obama visited Mari in Flint, and he decided that she was right, the old pipes needed to be replaced right away! He gave the city of Flint $100 million dollars from the government to repair its water system!

You might not know right now how you want to help fight climate change, but thinking about the things you care about most is a great way to start. Maybe you want to help animals, work on cleaning up beaches and the ocean, join other kids in telling government and business leaders to do the right things, or plant more trees.

Write about or draw the things you care about a lot, that you'd like to take care of and protect.

At the end of the book, you'll have a chance to make a plan for how to help the Earth and the things you care most about.

CHAPTER 5

Eco-Smart Thinking

You've been learning a lot about our world and your feelings about climate change. Now let's learn about your thoughts. Did you know that your feelings and thoughts are connected?

Think again about the last time you had to learn something new—maybe it was a sport, or a musical instrument, or learning to ride a bike. Learning a new thing can be hard at first!

You might have said to yourself, "I'll never be good at this! All the other kids are better than me!" Since your feelings are connected to your thoughts, you may have felt sad, mad, frustrated, and maybe even wanted to quit.

Thoughts like these are called unhelpful thoughts. You are telling yourself that you are not good enough and will fail. But that's not true!

There's good news! You can learn to replace these **unhelpful thoughts** with **helpful** thoughts.

What if instead, you told yourself, "It's hard to learn something new, but with practice I can get better. My coach told me I was doing well. Most kids find it hard at first. I want to keep learning and practicing, it's worth it."

Circle the feelings that match the helpful thoughts.

HOPEFUL   STRONG   accepting

patient   THANKFUL   INSPIRED

calmer   BOLD   RELAXED

determined   confident   trusting

encouraged

Helpful thinking is truer, and gives us patience, encouragement, and courage to keep learning.

Remember the What-Ifs from Chapter Three? Those are also types of unhelpful thoughts. Let's learn how to change those kinds of thoughts into eco-smart helpful ones!

Here are two examples of unhelpful thoughts about climate change. Circle the answer that is helpful eco-smart thinking.

1. Unhelpful: I can't do anything about climate change.

   A. I'm too young so I can't help.

   B. I can learn ways to improve our environment every day, like turning off the water faucet when I'm not using it.

3. Because of climate change, one day my home will be under water.

   A. Floods are part of climate change, but they don't happen everywhere. I can learn more about where I live and prepare for emergencies. I can do my part to protect people and places at home, in my community, and around the world.

   B. I will lose everything I care about.

If you picked B for question 1, and then A for question 2, you're right! Those are helpful eco-smart ways of thinking.

Here are two more examples of unhelpful thoughts that some kids have about climate change. **Write out** an eco-smart thought that is more helpful and truer.

1. Unhelpful: Nobody is doing anything to make our world safer and healthier.

   Your helpful eco-smart thought:

   _____

   _____

   _____

   _____

   _____

2. Unhelpful: We all need to be scientists to stop climate change.

   Your helpful eco-smart thought:

   _____

   _____

   _____

   _____

   _____

There are many correct eco-smart answers. If you weren't sure what to write, here are a few ideas to go along with yours.

1. Lots of people are working hard to solve climate change. Have you read about any?

2. Everyone has a way to help the Earth, including kids like you. All around the world there are teachers, doctors, parents, business owners, and many others working to make things better.

As long as the Earth needs our help to get back in balance from climate change, sometimes you're going to feel upset about it. Those feelings are like an alarm clock—they are there to help wake us up and remind us to make good choices for ourselves and the environment. Even though these worries are natural, they don't have to be with you all of the time.

Another way to outsmart unhelpful thinking is to have a **special worry time.**

With your special worry time, you set aside 15 minutes each day just for worrying. It's also good to pick a special worry place, like your favorite chair or a good place for drawing. A good time to have your worry time is after school (but not just before bedtime). Would 4:00 work? Or just after dinner?

Check with a parent and write down your best daily worry time.

_____

Where you will have your worry time?

_____

If any worry thoughts come to you at a different time—in the morning, at school, or at night in your bed—remind yourself, "I can worry about this later, during my special worry time." At those times, imagine those worries floating on a magic carpet to your worry shelf or drawer. They can rest there until your next special worry time.

To start your special worry time:

▶ Set a timer for 15 minutes.

▶ Let yourself think about all those worries that came up during the day or night. They can ride the magic carpet to join you for your 15 minute worry time.

▶ You can write, draw, or think about your worries.

▶ If a parent is free to join you, you can talk about your worries.

► Once the timer goes off, it's time to send away your worries again until tomorrow.

► You can put any worry drawings or writing on a special shelf or in a drawer until the next day.

As you practice your worry time, you may notice you have fewer and fewer worries at other times during the day or night!

Now take three deep breaths and imagine you are breathing in your favorite color! It's time do things that are fun or relaxing.

The WE CAN DO IT! Maze

Find your way through the maze and see if you find the eco-smart thoughts and feelings sign posts that will guide us to success in dealing with climate change.

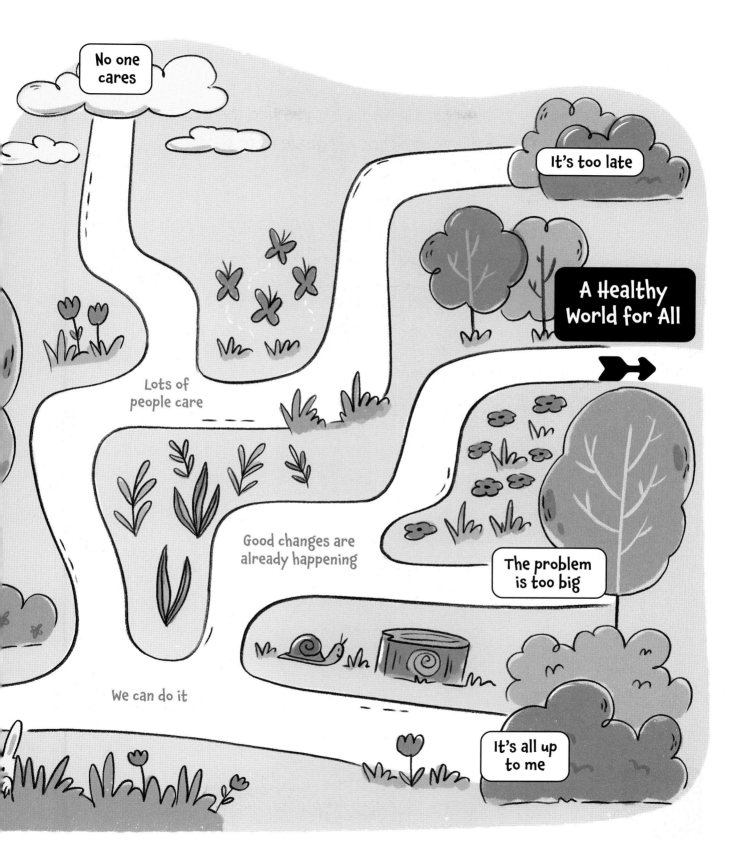

CHAPTER 6

That's Not Fair!

You're learning some great ways to feel calm and strong when you think about climate change and how it's affecting

plants, animals, and people,

sky, oceans, and rivers—

all the connected parts of our living world.

But climate change doesn't affect all the people and animals and places on Earth in the same way or the same amount. Some places are **really** affected, enough that human and animal homes are destroyed or it's unsafe to live somewhere. And some places haven't changed much.

It's OK to have strong feelings about that—and that's why people helping the environment also work toward **eco-justice**. "Eco" means the environment, and "justice" means treating everyone fairly.

So "eco-justice" means that *everyone* should have a chance to live in the healthiest and safest environment possible, with clean water and air, no matter the color of their skin, where they were born, or how much money they have.

You might already know that **racism** is when people are treated unfairly because of the color of their skin or sometimes what country they come from. **Environmental racism** means that pollution and climate change are often more serious and harmful in places where people of color live.

And that's not a coincidence! Polluting factories, power plants, and freeways are often built right in the communities where people of color have lived for generations.

For example, Black Americans, Indigenous People (the original people who lived in an area, like Native Americans), and other people of color make up a little bit less than half of everyone in the United States. But *much more than half* of the people who work, live, and play in the places with the worst air pollution are Black, indigenous, and other people of color.

That's not right, and it's not fair! This is one of the problems that eco-justice is trying to correct.

When you read about environmental injustice—how some people are treated unfairly—how does it make you feel? Have *you* ever been treated unfairly?

When I read about people being treated unfairly, I feel:

_____

_____

Eco-justice is important because: _____

_____

_____

Just being *aware* of eco-justice is a great first step toward making a difference. What else can you do?

One thing that really makes a big difference is including others when you're taking good care of yourself.

For example, solar panels are a good choice for producing clean energy. If your family owns a home and can put solar panels on the roof, that's great! But what if the people in your town got together and supported a big solar farm that made clean energy for the whole community?

That's a wonderful form of eco-justice, because everyone in all the different neighborhoods would benefit from clean, non-polluting energy.

Draw symbols from the list below on the best places to add community improvements to the map. For example, all neighborhoods need shade trees and the clean air that they produce: If you add trees in the places that don't have many, that's a great eco-justice choice.

 PLANT TREES

PUBLIC TRANSPORTATION

BIKE LANES

PARKS

CLEAN-AIR LAWS

COMMUNITY GARDENS

PUBLIC RECYCLING

Meet Aslan

Aslan Tudor is a Lipan Apache, and when he was eight years old, he travelled from Indianapolis, Indiana, to Standing Rock, North Dakota, with his family. They joined the Native American people living there who were working to stop an oil pipeline from being built across their land.

The pipeline is a long underground tube that carries fossil fuel oil. To build it, the oil company would have to dig up and destroy many special and beautiful places that the local people have loved and taken care of for thousands of years. The pipeline could also pollute their water supply and cause health problems to the Native Americans living there.

When Aslan was ten, he was surprised that many of his friends had never heard of Standing Rock, and his mom encouraged him to write about it. He loved books and reading, so he decided to write his own book: *Young Water Protectors: A Story About Standing Rock*. His mom helped him fill in a few details, and he described writing a book as "kind of hard, but fun." He's glad that many more people now know about the Standing Rock people's success at saving their sacred sites.

My Climate Book

Here are a few ideas to get your book started. This can be a story of something you hope to do soon. But write the story as if you already did it, and you are telling people about it. Imagine the most exciting project you'd like to do to help the Earth.

Title: _____

_____

By: _____

Fill in the lines of your Climate Story.

I'm happy to tell you that this year we _____

and _____ to help stop climate change.

To make this eco-smart change, I worked with _____

and _____ . They were really helpful because they

_____

_____

_____ .

It's great having climate partners.

What I love most about helping the planet is _____ .

Sometime it's hard because _____ .

If I still get sad or scared about climate change sometimes, what helps me

the most are _____ , _____ , and _____ .

Someone new I'd like to invite to join me in my next climate project is

_____ .

It's great to see what others are doing too.

One thing my family is doing to take good care of the Earth is _____

_____.

One thing my school is doing to take good care of the Earth is _____

_____.

I'm happy to know my community has started to _____.
Together we are strong!

One thing I feel really proud of is_____.

My strength comes from_____.

When I imagine a future with even more people helping create healthy

skies, oceans, and land, I feel _____.

Writing and talking about climate change can help us share ideas about how to make things better. We can inspire each other to think about the world in new ways and look at what's possible. Just imagine if you showed one friend an earth-friendly action that you're doing, like composting food waste, and they decided to do the same at their house. And then they tell their friends who try it out and tell others too. It's a great way to spread change!

CHAPTER 7

Be Prepared!

Do you practice fire drills at school? Every school, hospital, hotel, and other building always has a safety plan.

In our changing world, it's smart to have a safety plan for your home, too. Even before climate change, it was always good to know what to do in case of a fire, flood, earthquake, or any other emergency. It can help you feel calmer and safer if you have what you need and know what to do and where to go in an urgent situation.

In a fire drill, you practice going to a safe place outside. Depending on where you live and the kinds of emergencies you might face, you and your family should have a plan for a safe meeting place, too. Different emergencies call for different plans.

If there's a fire in your house, it makes sense to have a safe meeting place away from the house, just like in your school fire drill. But if it's stormy and windy outside, the best plan may be to have a cozy place inside your house to wait it out.

Ask to meet with your parents and **create a safety plan together. Together draw** a map of two of your safe meeting places and how to get there. Here is an example:

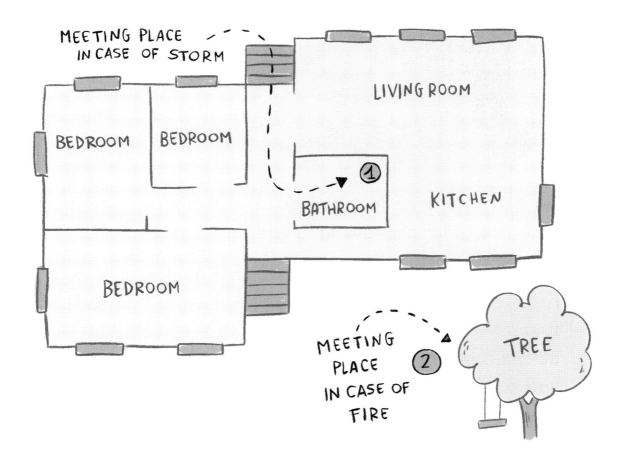

Draw a map of two of your safe meeting places and how to get there.

In case of a storm, our safe place is _____.

In case of a fire, our safe place is _____.

Another great way to be prepared is to make a **safety kit**. Your family's safety kit can have all the things you'll need in an emergency.

For example: if the power goes out during a storm, wouldn't it be great to have a flashlight nearby until the lights come back on? A flashlight is one of the more helpful things you can add to your home safety kit.

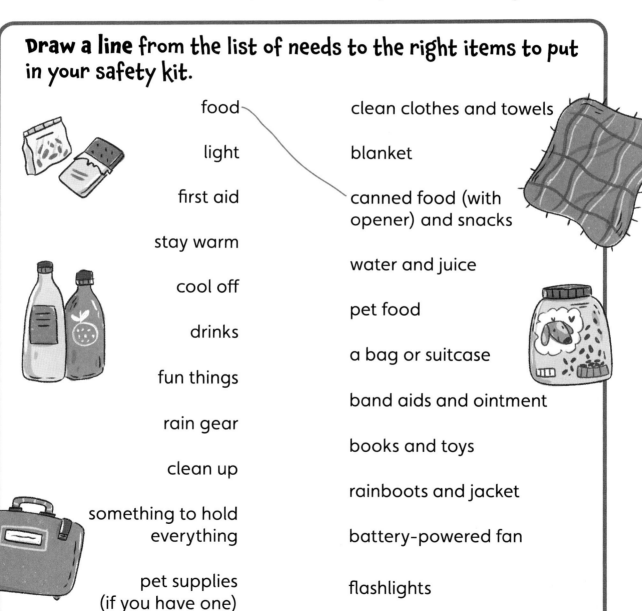

Draw a line from the list of needs to the right items to put in your safety kit.

food	clean clothes and towels
light	blanket
first aid	canned food (with opener) and snacks
stay warm	water and juice
cool off	pet food
drinks	a bag or suitcase
fun things	band aids and ointment
rain gear	books and toys
clean up	rainboots and jacket
something to hold everything	battery-powered fan
pet supplies (if you have one)	flashlights

Draw or write any other things that might be good to keep in your safety kit.

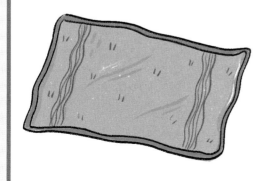

While you and your family are staying safe during an emergency, all kinds of helpers are working hard as a team to take care of your home and your community.

Firefighters, community centers with food and shelter, doctors and nurses, the energy company, and the police and sheriff all know exactly what to do if your town has an emergency.

You and your family are now prepared to take good care of yourselves—and here's something you can do to take care of your feelings, too. You don't have to pack it in a bag, it can travel with you anywhere and any time. It's called the **Butterfly Hug**.

Give it a try.

► Cross your arms over your chest with the tips of your fingers pointing toward the sky.

► Let them rest where you can feel your collarbones, those firm bony ridges across the top of your chest just below your shoulders.

► Now hook your thumbs together to form the body of a butterfly.

► Your hands and fingers will be its wings.

► Your eyes can be closed or partly closed looking down toward the ground.

► Begin to lift each wing one at a time while the butterfly body rests on your chest.

► Feel the tips of the wings tapping against your collarbones—right, left, right, left, right—very light and relaxed.

► While your butterfly gently taps, remember one of your favorite places where you feel relaxed and safe and imagine that you are there. Is it a quiet place where you can rest? Or a big place to run and play? Is there a pet or a certain person you want to have with you? Picture it just the way you want it right now while your butterfly tap, tap, taps a little more.

► Then rest your arms and open your eyes. How do you feel?

Make a drawing of your own butterfly that's always ready to give you a hug.

Being part of your family's plan to take good care of your home by creating the safety kit and meeting places, and giving your feelings a Butterfly Hug whenever they want one, is super smart planning. Great work!

CHAPTER 8

Working Together

You've learned a lot about taking care of yourself, your feelings, your thoughts, and your environment. And you're not the only one! Every day around the world, people of all ages are discovering ways to take better care of themselves and all the green and growing plants and amazing animals on our beautiful planet. We've already met two eco-heroes, Milo and Aslan. Let's meet a few more.

Stronger Together

One of the best ways to grow your climate superpowers is working together with others. Let's look at a few examples of kids making BIG eco-wise changes working together with their schools and communities.

The Green Bronx Machine started at Benjamin Franklin School in South Bronx, New York where schoolwork includes growing and cooking sustainable, healthy food! They have built gardens right on the school yard. They like to say they are "Growing a Greener World." The kids even get to take home bags of groceries every week.

So far, they have grown more than 100,000 pounds of vegetables, and they also share extra food with people in their community. Others have heard about this climate-friendly school, and now there are Green Machines in 20 states, and five other countries with school gardens.

Treasure Village Montessori school is in the Florida Keys, surrounded by the Atlantic Ocean. The kids and teachers learned that the beautiful coral reefs and marine ecosystems around their village were struggling because of climate change, and they decided to do something about it.

The school joined with a community organization called Celebration of the Sea Foundation. Together they created the Ocean Heroes program, where students work with teachers, scientists, and community leaders to help restore and protect the marine habitat.

Kids do lots of ocean projects for school, like removing plastic and invasive plants from the water. Ocean Heroes are working to create a sustainable future for our planet.

Helping My Community

Have **an adult help you draw** a simple map of your community. It doesn't need to match exactly where things are or include everything. You can include things like parks, libraries, factories, stores, a hospital, your school, and bike paths. Do you live by a lake, river, or ocean? Are there mountains or forests? And don't forget your home!

Once you have drawn your community, look again and find one or two places where you would like to help create a healthier world for all living creatures. **Draw a star** by them, and write about the projects you'd like to do.

It could be something like a litter pick up, planting trees, or safe places to ride a bike instead of riding in a car. Maybe there is an organization that helps the local animals, or a nature center with community projects. Is there a place you'd like to visit on a class field trip to learn more about helping the environment?

Draw the places and changes you'd like to help with, and **draw a star** by them.

Meet _____

Write in your name

One person's actions aren't going to fix climate change. If everyone does their part, *together* we can make the big changes that the planet needs.

There are all kinds of ways, large and small, to make a difference. Learn more about your community's efforts to fight climate change and see if there's something you can join—like going with a group to pick up litter or plant trees. At school, suggest a field trip to a nature or recycling center, do a class project on caring for the ocean, draw a poster for your classroom that shows wind and solar energy at work. What's important is to choose activities that you're excited about.

What changes or projects do you want to start in your community?

_____

_____.

Who can help you? _____

_____

_____.

When do you want to begin? _____

_____

_____.

What supplies do you need? _____

_____

_____.

Who will it help? _____

_____

_____.

What an exciting learning journey! Here is a collection of your new tools and activities that can help you be an eco-hero. Let's put your favorite ones in your eco-backpack so that they are easy to have with you whenever you want them. You've learned so much!

1. **Circle 5 or 6 of your favorite tools** that you will use most.

2. **Draw a picture** of your *favorite* tools in your backpack using a simple shape. For example, if you pick Nature Art as one of your favorites, you might draw a leaf or acorn, even though you used more objects in your picture. If you pick My What-If Chart, you could draw one thing that you wrote about. If you were worried about a storm, you could draw rain clouds, or being safely inside your home.

CHAPTER ONE
* *Three Hearts: Love of Nature, Curious About Climate Change, My Worries*

CHAPTER TWO
* *Nature Art*
* *Learn Climate Science*
* *My Feeling Body*

CHAPTER THREE
* *Ordinary and Fun Things*
* *What-If Chart*
* *Favorite Ways to Relax*

CHAPTER FOUR
* *My Feeling Garden*
* *Learning From Change*

CHAPTER FIVE
* *Eco-Smart Thinking*
* *My Worry Time*
* *We Can Do It! Maze*

CHAPTER SIX
* *Eco-Justice*
* *My Climate Book*

CHAPTER SEVEN
* *Emergency Preparation*
* *Butterfly Hug*

CHAPTER EIGHT
* *Being an Eco-Hero*
* *My Action Plan*
* *Team Work*

You might think that adding so many things to your backpack would make it very heavy. But like magic, this one feels lighter and lighter the more you put in it! That's because when you're prepared and take good care of your body, thoughts, and feelings, and you join with other people to take care of the Earth, you'll feel happier, more playful, and less worried. You'll feel...lighter!

Take a deep breath in and congratulate yourself on everything you've learned. Breathe out and feel confident and strong as one of many eco-heroes. I expect that you'll be meeting lots more as you continue your journey on our beautiful Earth.

Acknowledgments

Thanks to my family, who have always been some of my best teachers. Two strong child advocates reviewed a draft of the manuscript and offered valuable feedback: Jenni Silverstein, a Licensed Social Worker and Infant-Family Mental Health specialist who works at the intersection of Climate Justice and Early Childhood Mental Health, and Nancy Dunn, past president of the Fairfield-Suisun Unified Teachers Association and an elected Governing Board Trustee of the Vacaville Unified School District. Thank you for your wise perspectives and the gift of your time to support our kids.

Much gratitude for everyone on the Magination Press team who envisioned and helped shape this book. Katie Ten Hagen helped me write clearly to the kids so that they can navigate the challenges of climate change a little more easily. Illustrator Irma Ruggiero brought the ideas to life engaging the hearts and minds of the readers with her images.

And a very special thanks to Madeleine Fahrenwald, who somehow knows what I'm trying to say even if it's not yet on paper—and helps me say it.

About the Author, Illustrator, and Magination Press

Leslie Davenport is a climate psychology educator, consultant, and therapist exploring the intersectionality of climate, mental health, education, policy, and social justice. Leslie helped shape the document: "Mental Health and Our Changing Climate: Impacts, Implications, and Guidance" and authored four books including *Emotional Resiliency in the Era of Climate Change*, and *All the Feelings Under the Sun*, a Magination Press book for tweens. She is an advisor to Post Carbon Institute, Climate Mental Health Network, One Resilient Earth. She is faculty and program lead of the Climate Psychology Certification at the California Institute of Integral Studies. Visit lesliedavenport.com.

Irma Ruggiero is an Italian illustrator and author. In 2020, she graduated from the Academy of Fine Arts in Naples with an illustrated project-book for visually impaired children. Later, she earned a degree in Illustration from the Italian School of Comix. For now she lives in Rome, but who knows in the future! Visit behance.net/irmaruggiero and @irma_illustra on Instagram.

Magination Press is the children's book imprint of the American Psychological Association. APA works to advance psychology as a science and profession and as a means of promoting health and human welfare. Magination Press books reach young readers and their parents and caregivers to make navigating life's challenges a little easier. It's the combined power of psychology and literature that makes a Magination Press book special. Visit maginationpress.org and @MaginationPress on Facebook, Instagram, X, and Pinterest.